Grace the Glitter Fairy

To Ellie Delamere, who loves fairies

Special thanks to

Narinder Dhami

ISBN 978-0-545-26690-1

12 11 10 9 8 7 6 5 4 3 2 1   10 11 12 13 14 15/0

Printed in the U.S.A.   40

First Scholastic Book Clubs printing, September 2010

Grace
the Glitter
Fairy

by Daisy Meadows

LITTLE APPLE

SCHOLASTIC INC.

New York   Toronto   London   Auckland
Sydney   Mexico City   New Delhi   Hong Kong

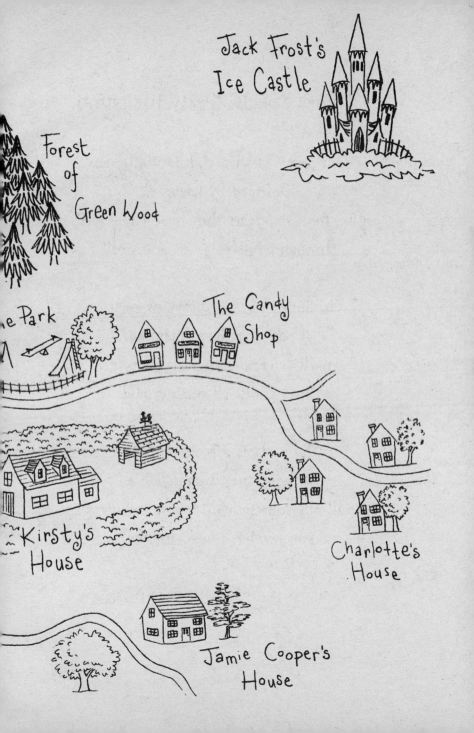

A Very Special Party Invitation

Our gracious king and gentle queen
Are loved by fairies all.
One thousand years they have ruled well,
Through troubles great and small.

In honor of their glorious reign
A party has been planned.
We'll celebrate their anniversary
Throughout all of Fairyland.

The party is a royal surprise,
We hope they'll be delighted.
So pull out your fanciest wand and dress . . .
For *you* have been invited!

RSVP: THE FAIRY GODMOTHER

Contents

A Party Plan

"Isn't it a beautiful day?" Kirsty Tate said
happily, looking up at the deep blue sky.
"I'm so glad you're staying here for a
whole week, Rachel."

Kirsty was sitting on the grass in the
Tates' backyard, making a daisy chain
with her best friend, Rachel Walker. Pearl,
Kirsty's black-and-white kitten, was

snoozing in a patch of sunshine in the middle of the path.

"You know, Rachel," Kirsty went on, picking another daisy. "This is the perfect day for—"

"A party!" Rachel broke in, knowing exactly what Kirsty was going to say.

Kirsty nodded. A frown came over her face. "Let's hope Jack Frost's goblins don't spoil someone's special day."

"The Party Fairies will do their best to stop them," Rachel replied, sounding determined. "And so will we."

Rachel and Kirsty had a wonderful secret that no one else in the human world knew about. They were best friends with the fairies! The girls had helped many different fairies when Jack Frost caused trouble with his evil spells. Now they were working with the Party Fairies.

"Isn't it just like Jack Frost to want to ruin everyone's fun?" said Kirsty. "He just can't stop being mischievous."

"If he wasn't always so mean, he could have come to the surprise party for the fairy king and queen's 1000th anniversary," Rachel pointed out.

The girls had been invited to the Fairyland party by the Fairy Godmother, and they had been very excited about it—until they found out that Jack Frost was determined to have a party of his own. His goblins were causing trouble at human parties. The goblins planned to steal the fairies' magic party bags when the Party Fairies showed up to fix the party problems. Then the goblins were going to take the party bags to Jack Frost, so he could use them at his party.

"Well, we managed to keep Cherry the Cake Fairy and Melodie the Music Fairy's party bags safe," Kirsty said, adding another daisy to her chain. "We'll just have to keep our eyes open."

"And our ears," added Rachel.

Suddenly, there was a rustling behind the fence. "OW!" someone muttered. "That hurt."

"Who was that?" Rachel gasped. "Do you think it was a goblin?"

Kirsty grinned and shook her head. "It's OK," she said. "It sounds like Mr. Cooper, our next-door neighbor."

At that moment, Mr. Cooper popped his head over the fence. He was a tall, thin man with a cheerful smile. "Sorry, Kirsty," he said, "did I startle you?

I pricked my finger on the rosebush."
He held up a small package wrapped
in shiny blue paper. "I'm trying to hide
these presents around our yard for the
treasure hunt this afternoon."

"Treasure hunt?" repeated Rachel,
looking confused.

Mr. Cooper nodded. "Yes, it's my son
Jamie's birthday today," he replied. "He's
five, and we're having a party."

A party! Rachel and Kirsty glanced at each other in excitement.

"We have ten kids coming," Mr. Cooper went on. "And we've hired a clown named Mr. Chuckles. Jamie is really excited." He smiled and shook his head. "It's going to be a lot of hard work, though."

Rachel nudged Kirsty, who knew exactly what her friend was thinking.

"Maybe Rachel and I could come over and give you and Mrs. Cooper some help?" Kirsty suggested.

"Yes, we'd love to," Rachel added eagerly.

Mr. Cooper's face lit up. "That's very nice of you," he said. "Jamie would love that. The guests are arriving at three o'clock, so could you come at two?"

"Of course," Rachel and Kirsty said together.

Mr. Cooper gave them a grateful smile, and went off to hide some more packages.

Kirsty turned to Rachel, her eyes wide with excitement. "Do you think a goblin will show up and try to make trouble at Jamie's party?" she asked.

"I don't know," Rachel replied. "But if one does, we'll be ready for him!"

Decorating Difficulties

"This is going to be fun!" Kirsty grinned as she rang the Coopers' doorbell. "Jamie is really sweet. It'll be kind of noisy with him and all his friends running around and having a good time, though."

"Maybe they'll scare the goblins away!" Rachel said with a laugh.

The front door opened. A small boy with the same cheerful smile as Mr. Cooper stood in the hallway.

"Hi, Kirsty," Jamie called eagerly. "Are you and your friend here to help with my party?"

"Yes, we are," Kirsty replied, smiling and handing Jamie a small present. "Happy birthday."

Jamie tore off the wrapping paper and smiled when he saw the bright red car inside. "Thank you! Come on in," he said, taking Kirsty's hand. "Me and Mommy are putting up decorations in the family room."

Rachel and Kirsty followed him down the hallway. Mrs. Cooper was standing on a chair, pinning a HAPPY BIRTHDAY banner to the wall.

"Hello, Kirsty!" She smiled. "And Rachel, right? It's so nice of you to help out. Thank you."

"Mom!" Jamie was dancing around the family room, waving his new car. "Look what Kirsty and Rachel gave me! And can we put up the streamers now? Can we?"

"There's still an hour to go and he's already bursting with excitement," Mrs. Cooper said, laughing. "Do you think you girls could put up the streamers and balloons, while I go and help Jamie's dad finish up the food?" She pointed to a folded, glittery paper tablecloth, and some bowls and plates that were on the table. "And if you have time, could you set the table, too?"

"Absolutely," Rachel replied.

Mrs. Cooper thanked the girls and hurried to the kitchen.

Jamie grabbed the box of decorations from the sofa. "Daddy bought some new extra-long streamers," Jamie said proudly. "They're gold and silver—look!"

He began unrolling one of the streamers. But before he got very far, a piece no more than two feet long dropped off and floated to the ground.

"Oh!" Jamie gasped.

"I'm sure the rest of the roll is fine," Rachel said quickly. "Keep going, Jamie."

But as Jamie unrolled the streamer, more short pieces of brightly-colored paper fell off. Rachel opened the other packets, but those streamers were ruined, too. "It looks like someone cut the streamers into lots of pieces and then rolled them back up again," Kirsty whispered to Rachel.

Rachel nodded. "Do you think it could be goblin mischief?" she asked with a frown on her face.

Jamie looked as if he were close to

tears. "They're too short!" he wailed.

"Don't worry, Jamie," Kirsty said, giving him a hug. "I know just the thing to fix this. I'll be right back."

Kirsty ran home and found a big roll of sparkly, blue tape that was left over from Christmas. Then she went back to the Coopers' house and showed it to Jamie. "Look," she said, beginning to stick the pieces of one of the streamers together. "Now you'll have striped gold, silver, *and* blue streamers."

Jamie's face lit up. "They look even better now!" he declared happily.

The three of them quickly stuck the rest of the streamers together, and then Rachel and Kirsty began to pin them up around the room. They had just finished when the doorbell rang.

"That should be Mr. Chuckles," Mrs. Cooper called from the kitchen. "Could you let him in, please, Kirsty?"

"I think Jamie beat me to it!" Kirsty laughed as Jamie raced past her into the hall.

Rachel and Kirsty followed him, and found the clown standing on the doorstep, smiling down at Jamie. He wore a bright blue, baggy suit and a blue hat.

"You must be the birthday boy," he said.

"Where's your big red nose and your big clown shoes, Mr. Chuckles?" Jamie wanted to know. Rachel and Kirsty smiled.

"Ah, well, I'm not quite ready yet," Mr. Chuckles explained. "It's difficult to drive my van in big clown shoes."

Looking as if he might explode with excitement, Jamie ran to tell his mom about the clown.

Meanwhile, Mr. Chuckles turned to Rachel and Kirsty. "Is it OK if I set up my stuff in the family room?" he asked.

Kirsty nodded. "Yes, we're almost finished decorating," she replied. "We just have to put up the balloons."

The clown opened the back of his van and began to unload his props, while the girls went back into the family room. But they groaned when they saw that the streamers had all fallen down! Now they were in piles on the floor.

"This has to be the work of one of Jack Frost's goblins!" Rachel said, scowling and grabbing a streamer. "He must be here somewhere."

"Quick, let's get these back up — or Jamie will be upset," Kirsty said, picking up the tape.

The girls worked fast. They got the streamers back in place before Jamie came bouncing into the room.

"We're going to blow up the balloons now, Jamie," said Kirsty, opening one of the packets. "Which color should we start with?"

"Gold!" Jamie answered immediately.

Kirsty began to blow air into the long gold balloon. But even though she huffed and puffed and got red in the face, the balloon wouldn't inflate. It stayed as flat as a pancake!

"There's a hole in it," Rachel said, looking closely at the balloon.

The girls glanced at each other. They were both thinking exactly the same thing.

"The goblin again!" Kirsty whispered.
Quickly, she and Rachel checked the
other balloons.
There were holes
in all of them!
Jamie's bottom lip
was trembling.
"Are there any
balloons we can blow
up? Are they all ruined?"
he asked in a small voice.

At that moment, Mr. Chuckles came
into the room carrying a big wooden
box. "Did I hear you need balloons?" he
asked. "I've got extra." He put his hand
into his pocket and pulled out a handful
of different-colored balloons. "I use them
to make my balloon animals."

Kirsty and Rachel were very relieved to see Jamie smiling again. Quickly, they blew up the balloons and hung them around the French doors—beautiful, tall doors with windows from top to bottom—at the far end of the room.

Suddenly, the doorbell rang. Jamie peeked out of the front window. "It's Matthew, my best friend!" he shouted excitedly. "And Katie and Andy and Ben. It's time for my party to start!" He dashed out to meet his guests.

"Look at the time! I need to go to the bathroom and put my clown makeup on," said Mr. Chuckles. He grabbed a small case and left the room.

POP! POP! POP!

Kirsty and Rachel jumped and turned around. The balloons they had just put up were bursting, one by one!

"I'm getting sick of that goblin,"
Rachel said.

"So am I," Kirsty agreed. "We need to
find him and put a stop to his tricks!"

The doorbell was ringing again as
more guests arrived. The girls could hear
them chatting excitedly in the hall. There
wasn't much time to find and stop the
goblin.

Then they heard Mr.
Cooper's voice. "Follow
me to the backyard,
kids," he was saying.
"We're going to have
a treasure hunt!"

There was a loud
cheer as the kids
hurried after him. Rachel and Kirsty
looked at each other with relief.

"Let's search the room," Kirsty suggested. "We might be able to catch the goblin while everyone's in the backyard."

But just as they began their search, Rachel gasped in surprise and clutched Kirsty's arm.

"What is it?" Kirsty whispered.

"Look!" Rachel said, pointing toward the French doors. "Outside in the garden."

Kirsty stared through the glass and saw something sparkly and pink flying swiftly through the air. It was zooming straight through the backyard,

toward the French doors of the family room.

"Oh!" Kirsty cried. "It's Grace the Glitter Fairy!"

"Yes," said Rachel anxiously. "And the kids are going out to the backyard. They'll all see her unless we do something—and fast!"

Saving Grace

"We have to go outside and warn her," Kirsty said.

"But what about the goblin?" Rachel asked.

"This is more important," Kirsty replied, opening the French doors. She and Rachel rushed outside, waving their arms all around to get Grace's attention.

Grace saw the girls right away and waved her sparkling wand at them. She had long, straight, glossy blond hair, and she wore a glittering pink dress, which shimmered in the sunshine. The hem of the dress was red and cut into a zigzag pattern.

"Hello, girls," she called. "It's good to see you—"

"Grace, you have to hide!" Kirsty burst out, without even saying hello. "The party guests are about to go out to the backyard any second!"

Before Grace could say anything, they heard the back door open.

"So that's what you have to do, kids," Mr. Cooper was saying. "Ready, set, go!"

Grace looked alarmed as all the children came rushing out the back door. She fluttered out of sight behind a garden urn filled with flowers—just in time!

The children were running all around the garden now, screaming with excitement. Two little girls came over to

where Kirsty and Rachel were standing, and began to search for presents there.

"Um, I think Mr. Cooper hid most of the presents toward the back by the fence," Rachel said quickly. She didn't want the little girls poking around and finding Grace.

One of the girls ran off right away, but the other one frowned. "I see something sparkly behind that pot," she said stubbornly, pointing at the urn. "It might be one of the presents."

"Oh, no," Kirsty said, thinking fast. She bent down and picked Grace up, keeping the fairy out of sight in her hand. Then she put her hand—and Grace—in her pocket. "That's just an empty candy wrapper."

"We'll put it in the trash can with the garbage," Rachel added.

The girl looked disappointed and ran off after her friend. Kirsty and Rachel sighed with relief.

"Garbage?" Grace said, poking her head out of Kirsty's pocket. She looked a little flustered and her hair was all messy. "Thanks a lot!"

"Sorry, Grace," Kirsty said soothingly. "We didn't mean it."

"There's a goblin here," Rachel told Grace, as the little fairy smoothed her hair. "He's been ruining all the party decorations in the house."

"Well, we'll put a stop to that!" Grace declared, looking outraged. "Where is he?"

"We don't know," Kirsty replied. "We were just about to start looking for him, when we saw you coming."

Grace nodded. "Now I can help you find him," she said, smiling. "Lead the way!"

As Kirsty led the way through the French doors into the family room, she suddenly grabbed Rachel's arm. "Look, there!" she whispered. "Behind the curtain."

Rachel and Grace peered at the long blue curtains hanging on either side of the French doors, and immediately saw what Kirsty had spotted. There was something behind one of them—and that something was shaped like a goblin!

An Uninvited Guest

They all stared at the goblin-shaped lump behind the curtain. They saw it move once or twice. The goblin was obviously getting a little antsy.

Kirsty motioned for Rachel and Grace to follow her to the other end of the room. "We need to do something right now," Kirsty whispered. "Before

Jamie and his friends come in from the backyard."

"Yes, but what?" Grace asked, biting her lip.

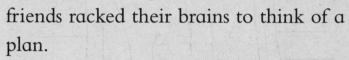

The three friends racked their brains to think of a plan.

"We could sneak up on the goblin and grab him while he's wrapped in the curtain," Rachel suggested. "It shouldn't be too tough. He's very small." Rachel knew that Jack Frost's magic could make the goblins much bigger and scarier when they were in the human world, but this goblin was his normal size. "Then Grace can quickly send him back to

Fairyland with magic," Rachel added.

Grace nodded enthusiastically, but Kirsty looked worried. "He'll try to fight his way out," she said. "What if he ruins the curtain?"

"Well, it's made of really thick material," Rachel pointed out. "I don't think the goblin will be able to do much damage."

"And I can fix it with fairy magic!" Grace added.

"OK, let's give it a try," Kirsty agreed.

She and Rachel crept cautiously toward the French doors, with Grace fluttering alongside them. They had

almost reached the goblin, when the
door between the kitchen and the family
room suddenly opened. Mrs. Cooper
appeared, carrying plates of food.

Quick as a flash,
Grace darted into
Kirsty's pocket, out
of sight.

"Oh, girls," said
Jamie's mom,
"could you give
me a hand with these snacks?"

Rachel and Kirsty were desperate to
catch the goblin, but there was nothing
they could do while Mrs. Cooper was in
the room.

"Yes, of course," Kirsty replied politely.
The girls hurried to help Mrs. Cooper set
down the plates on the dining table.

"As soon as the kids finish the treasure
hunt, we'll bring them in here," Mrs.
Cooper told the girls. "They can have a
snack before they watch Mr. Chuckles.

Then, after his show, we'll have cake."

The girls nodded and Mrs. Cooper headed back to the kitchen.

As soon as she had gone, Grace fluttered out of Kirsty's pocket. The girls turned back to tackle the goblin—but it was too late!

"Oh, no!" cried Rachel, as she looked around the room. All the streamers lay on the floor again. The decorations were ruined. But even worse, the goblin shape behind the curtain had disappeared!

"Well, at least I can fix these decorations," Grace

said, reaching into her pocket for her party bag.

But Kirsty stopped her. "No, you shouldn't do that," she said in a low voice. "That's exactly what the goblin wants you to do. I'm sure he's hiding somewhere—just waiting for the chance to steal your party bag!"

Goblin Trap!

At that very moment, the three friends heard a rustling noise behind the couch!

"The goblin must be hiding over there," Rachel whispered excitedly, pointing. "He must have heard us talking about the party bag."

Kirsty's face lit up. "That's it!" she whispered. "We'll use Grace's party bag

as bait to catch the goblin."

"I know how we can grab him, too," Rachel added quietly. She pointed at the paper tablecloth that Mrs. Cooper had bought for the party. "We'll wrap him up in the tablecloth instead of the curtain. Then Grace can still carry him off to Fairyland!"

"Good idea," Grace whispered. "If we hide behind that armchair, we'll catch him red-handed." Then she spoke again in a louder voice. "My party bag is so heavy, girls," she said with a wink. "It must be because I have so much magic fairy dust in it."

"Why don't you put it down on the coffee table?" Rachel suggested, glancing at the couch.

"Then you can come into the kitchen with us, and we'll show you Jamie's beautiful birthday cake," added Kirsty, picking up the shiny, gold-colored tablecloth. "It's shaped like a train."

"OK," Grace agreed. She pulled her sparkly pink party bag from her pocket, and placed it carefully on the coffee table. "We can go now."

But instead of leaving the room, they all tiptoed over to

the armchair and hid behind it. It was
a tight squeeze! Kirsty and Rachel were
too big to both fit behind the chair.

"Rachel, your feet are sticking out,"
Grace whispered. "Wait a minute."

She twirled her wand in the air and surrounded the girls with sparkling fairy dust. A moment later, Rachel and Kirsty had shrunk to fairy-size, with sparkly wings on their backs. As tiny fairies, it was easy for all three friends to fit behind the armchair. Kirsty fluttered her wings happily.

Grace looked pleased. "That's better," she said, glancing at the couch. "And we're just in time. Here he comes . . ."

The goblin poked his head around the corner of the couch to see if the coast was clear. Then he stepped out with a big grin on his mean face. His beady eyes gleamed as he spotted the party bag lying on the coffee table. He hurried to pick it up. "Jack Frost will be so happy with me," the goblin said smugly.

But as he reached for the party bag, Grace, Kirsty, and Rachel zoomed out of their hiding place, each holding a corner of the tablecloth.

"Get him!" Rachel yelled.

They hovered above the surprised goblin and dropped the tablecloth. He gave a shout of anger as it covered him completely from head to toe.

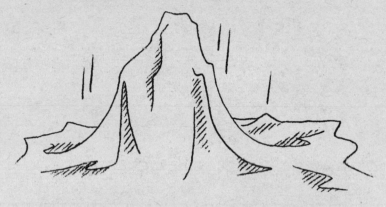

"It worked!" cried Kirsty.

"Now, let's wrap him up more tightly," Grace said.

But before they could do that, the goblin began to rip the tablecloth into shreds!

All Wrapped Up!

"He's tearing his way out!" Kirsty exclaimed. "What can we do?"

Rachel looked around, spotted the streamers on the floor, and got an idea. She grabbed the end of one of them, and flew swiftly around and around the goblin, tying him up.

"Quick, Kirsty!" Grace called, as she

saw what Rachel was doing. "Grab a
streamer."

"Stop it!" the goblin shouted angrily.
He tried to fight his way out, but Grace
and the girls were wrapping him up too
quickly. A few minutes later, he couldn't
move. He looked just like a mummy.

"Ohhh!" The goblin sulked.

"Serves you right," Rachel told him, as Grace rescued her party bag.

Meanwhile, Kirsty had fluttered over to the French doors to check on the treasure hunt.

"OK, kids, you've found all the presents," Mr. Cooper was saying. "Now it's time to have a snack and see Mr. Chuckles, the clown."

"Jamie and his friends are coming now, Grace," Kirsty called. "You'd better go."

Grace turned to the goblin. "And you're coming with me!" She laughed and waved her wand. The groaning, grumbling goblin disappeared in a cloud of sparkling fairy dust.

"Good–bye, girls, and thank you," Grace said. She gave them a hug and, with a wave of her wand, made them human-size again.

Then Kirsty remembered the decorations. "Grace, can you help?" she asked, pointing at the streamers and balloons.

Grace nodded and smiled. She opened her party bag and emptied all the fairy dust into the family room. Tiny, shining diamonds whirled and swirled around the room, spinning into every corner.

When the magic dust had cleared, Kirsty and Rachel were thrilled to see that glittering, rainbow-colored streamers and

balloons hung all around the room. There was even a new, gold tablecloth. When Kirsty and Rachel spread it out on the table, they saw that it was shinier than before and sprinkled with silver stars.

"Thank you!" the girls cried in amazement.

Grace gave them a beaming smile, waved her wand, and disappeared. Just then, the younger kids charged in, followed by Mr. Cooper. They all stopped and stared in amazement at the fabulous decorations.

"Wow!" Jamie gasped. "Look what Kirsty and Rachel did, Dad!"

"It's fantastic, girls," said Mr. Cooper gratefully.

Rachel and Kirsty winked at each other, grabbed a snack, and sat down with the party guests to watch Mr. Chuckles perform. The clown was very funny! He had everyone laughing at his giant, water-squirting sunflower. Rachel

and Kirsty enjoyed it just as much as Jamie and his friends.

At the end of the show, Mr. Chuckles told them he was going to make some balloon animals. When he opened his bag and pulled out a handful of balloons, there was a gasp of wonder. They were the most wonderful, colorful balloons anyone had ever seen—some

were even striped and spotted with animal-print designs!

Mr. Chuckles stared at the balloons in delight. "I didn't even know I had these," he muttered.

Rachel and Kirsty smiled. They knew where those balloons had come from—Grace the Glitter Fairy!

Mr. Chuckles began to twist and tie the balloons together. He made an elephant first, which he gave to Jamie. Then he made a giraffe and a zebra.

"These are for the two girls who put up these beautiful decorations," Mr.

Chuckles said. He bowed, and presented the giraffe to Rachel and the zebra to Kirsty. The girls were thrilled!

And they weren't the only ones . . .

"This is my best birthday ever!" Jamie

declared, as the clown began to make animals for all the other kids.

"And we've saved another Party Fairy and her party bag," Rachel whispered happily to Kirsty. "Hooray!"

Cherry, Melodie, and Grace
all have their magic party bags back.
Now Rachel and Kirsty must help

Honey
the Candy Fairy!

Join their next adventure
in this special sneak peek. . . .

A Trip to the Candy Shop

It was a beautiful, sunny day, and Mr. and Mrs. Tate had set the table for lunch outside in the yard. As Kirsty and her best friend, Rachel Walker, sat down to eat, Mrs. Tate suddenly groaned.

"I knew there was something else I meant to get from town this morning," she cried. "Toffees for Gran! I promised

I'd take her some tonight, and I completely forgot to buy them."

Kirsty put down her sandwich. "Don't worry, Mom. We'll go to Mrs. Twist's Candy Shop after lunch for you," she suggested. She glanced at Rachel. "What do you think?"

"Sure," Rachel said. "I always have time to go to the candy store!"

The two girls smiled at each other.

Rachel was staying with the Tates for a whole week. She and Kirsty had met when their families vacationed on Rainspell Island, and they had been best friends ever since. Somehow, whenever the girls got together, they always seemed to have the most wonderful adventures—fairy adventures!

"That reminds me," Mr. Tate said. "I

saw in the local newspaper that Mrs. Twist is retiring. Her daughter's taking over the candy store starting tomorrow. Since this is her last day, Mrs. Twist is throwing a party for all her customers." He winked at Kirsty and Rachel. "I read something about there being lots of free candy, too!"

Kirsty nudged Rachel. "Candy *and* a party," she repeated. "How exciting!"

"We love parties," Rachel agreed, with a grin.

RAINBOW magic™

There's Magic in Every Series!

The Rainbow Fairies

The Weather Fairies

The Jewel Fairies

The Pet Fairies

The Fun Day Fairies

The Petal Fairies

The Dance Fairies

The Music Fairies

The Sports Fairies

The Party Fairies

Read them all!

■SCHOLASTIC

www.scholastic.com

www.rainbowmagiconline.com

HIT entertainment

RMFAIR

RAINBOW magic™

SPECIAL EDITION

Three Books in One— More Rainbow Magic Fun!

■SCHOLASTIC

www.scholastic.com
www.rainbowmagiconline.com

HIT entertainment

RMSPECIAL3

RAINBOW magic

These activities are magical!
Play dress-up, send friendship notes, and much more!

SCHOLASTIC
www.scholastic.com
www.rainbowmagiconline.com

HiT entertainment

RMACTIV